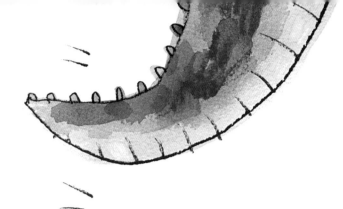

For my dad, Norman Kippes,
who always liked to be noticed
—T. S.

For Maurice Leutenegger
—L. S.

SIMON & SCHUSTER BOOKS FOR YOUNG READERS • An imprint of Simon & Schuster Children's Publishing Division • 1230 Avenue of the Americas, New York, New York 10020 • Text copyright © 2015 by Tammi Sauer • Illustrations copyright © 2015 by Liz Starin • All rights reserved, including the right of reproduction in whole or in part in any form. • SIMON & SCHUSTER BOOKS FOR YOUNG READERS is a trademark of Simon & Schuster, Inc. • For information about special discounts for bulk purchases, please contact Simon & Schuster • Special Sales at 1-866-506-1949 or business@simonandschuster.com. • The Simon & Schuster Speakers Bureau can bring authors to your live event. For more information or to book an event, contact the Simon & Schuster Speakers Bureau at 1-866-248-3049 or visit our website at www.simonspeakers.com. • Book design by Laurent Linn • The text for this book is set in Billy Std and 1751 GLC Copperplate. • The illustrations for this book are rendered in ink, watercolor, crayon, and colored pencil. • Manufactured in China • 0715 SCP • 10 9 8 7 6 5 4 3 2 1 • Library of Congress Cataloging-in-Publication Data • Sauer, Tammi. • Roar! / Tammi Sauer ; illustrated by Liz Starin. • pages cm • "A Paula Wiseman Book." • Summary: "A little boy is determined to prove that he is a dragon in this story about friendship and fitting in"—Provided by publisher. • ISBN 978-1-4814-0224-8 (hardcover : alk. paper) • ISBN 978-1-4814-0225-5 (eBook) • [1. Dragons—Fiction. 2. Friendship—Fiction.] I. Starin, Liz, illustrator. II. Title. • PZ7.S2502Ro 2014 • [E]—dc23 • 2013023836

first edition

ROAR!

Tammi Sauer

ILLUSTRATED BY
Liz Starin

A Paula Wiseman Book

SIMON & SCHUSTER BOOKS FOR YOUNG READERS

NEW YORK LONDON TORONTO SYDNEY NEW DELHI

Hmph.

I am **toothy** and I am **fierce**. See?

Actually, you are cute. Really cute.

Grr...

Let me get this straight.

Are you saying that I am **not** big,

I am **not** scary,

and I am **not** fire-breathing?

Yes!

Don't look
at me.

Sniff.

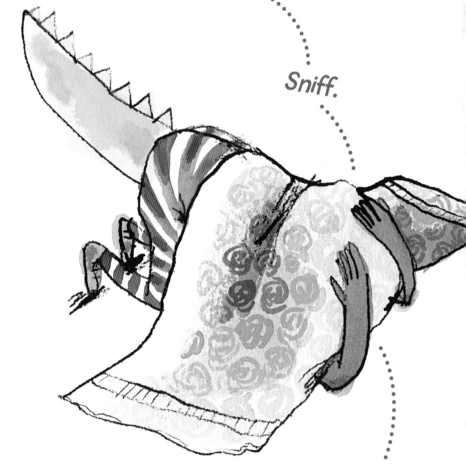

I am all wrong.

No, you're not.
There are lots
of things you
can do.

You can play hide-and-seek.

And turn cartwheels.

And eat ice cream!

Hmmm . . .

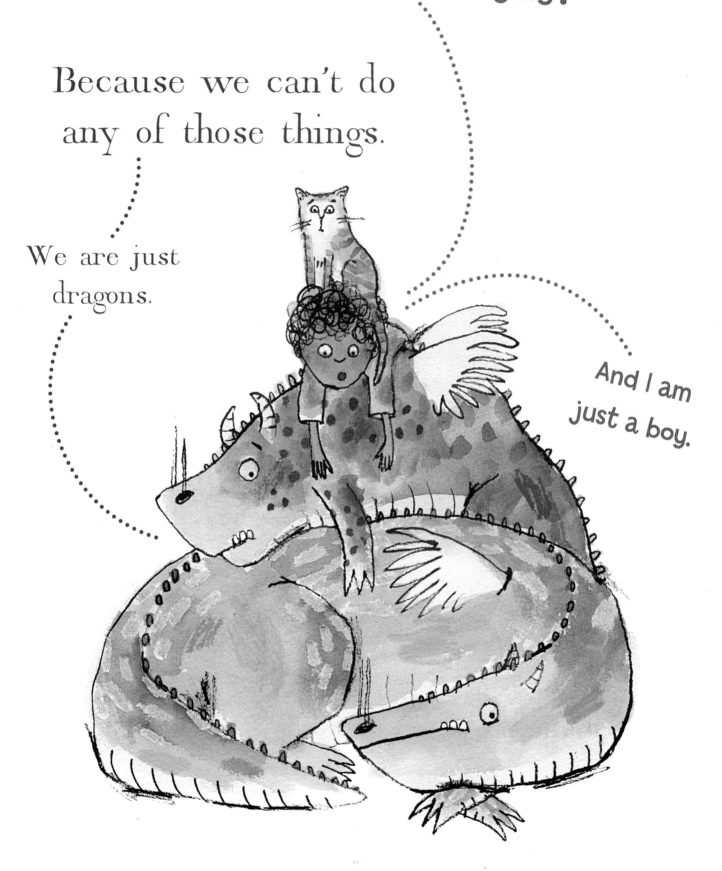

Can you make a silly face?

We *love* to make silly faces.

Then we are not just a boy and two dragons.

Look at us!

We are friends.